WILEY & GRAMPA'S CREATURE FEATURES

CURSE OF THE KITTY LITTER

WRITTEN AND ILLUSTRATED BY

KIRK SCROGGS

SMELL THE HORROR!

LITTLE, BROWN AND COMPANY
Books for Young Readers
New York   Boston

Special thanks to:
Steve Deline, Jackie Greed, Suppasak Viboonlarp, Mark Mayes,
Hiland Hall, Alejandra, Inge Govaerts, Joe Kocian, Jim Jeong, Frank Ortiz,
and Will Keightly.

A supernatural thanks to Andrea, Jill, Ames, Elizabeth, Saho, Maria, and
the Little, Brown Crew. Woo woo!

A creaky, cobweb-covered thanks to Ashley and Carolyn Grayson,
Christa and Andrea and the Mrs. Nelsons crew, and Dav Pilkey.

And a levitating, ectoplasmic thanks to Harold Aulds, Corey and
Candance, and Diane Scroggs.

Little, Brown and Company

Hachette Book Group USA
237 Park Avenue, New York, NY 10017
Visit our Web site at www.lb-kids.com

First Edition: August 2008

ISBN-13: 978-0-316-00690-3 / ISBN-10: 0-316-00690-4

10 9 8 7 6 5 4 3 2 1

CW

Printed in the United States of America

Series design by Saho Fujii

The illustrations for this book were done in Staedtler ink on Canson Marker paper,
then digitized with Adobe Photoshop for color and shade.
The text was set in Humana Sans Light and the display type was handlettered.

CHAPTERS

CHAPTER 1

Take a Whiff

Ladies and gentlemen, Swedish pastry chefs,
and connoisseurs of fine odors . . . A horrible
presence roams these halls. A ghoulish, gooey,
and sometimes gassy ghost that breaks furniture,
wails and moans like a hippo with a toothache, and
smells like a Limburger cheese and sauerkraut
quesadilla.

Turn back now! Your nostrils are in grave danger. . . .

Don't be frightened! Those aren't ghosts. It's just Gramma and Merle in their nightly avocado, cucumber, and cold-cream beauty masks.

"Hold it down in here!" yelled Gramma. "Merle and I are trying to get our beauty rest. Merle's gotta look his best for the Gingham County Cat Show this weekend."

"Sorry, Granny!" Grampa said. "But we just installed our new eleven-speaker surround-sound system. *Howl of The Poodle People* is coming on at midnight and I want the walls to shake with every shriek of terror."

CHAPTER 2

Bad News Bearers

Just then, the phone rang with the fury of a thousand angry trombones!

I answered it and got some very bad news.

"Grampa," I said sadly, "I'm afraid I've got some terrible news for you."

"They've cancelled *Wheel of Fortune*?" asked Grampa.

"No," I said. "Your fourth cousin-in-law, Lord Rankonstink, passed away in a tragic rabid aardvark incident and you've been left something in his will."

"Noooooo!" screamed Grampa as he swung from the chandelier and threw breakables. "Why does fate have to be so cruel?"

"Wow!" I said. "You guys must have been close."

"Actually, I didn't know I even had a fourth cousin-in-law," said Grampa. "I just felt like breaking something."

CHAPTER 3

Mind Your Manors

The next day we headed toward Lord Rankonstink's home. I even asked my best friend, Jubal, to come along.

"Are you kidding?" said Jubal. "It was either this or do my math homework."

GINGHAM COUNTY
CAT SHOW
NEXT SATURDAY!
CHECK IT OUT,
DAWG.

SPEED
LIMIT
95

Austin

We arrived at our destination, a ginormous, spooky, ramshackle mansion called Badtable Manor.

"Just think," said Grampa, "this could all be ours."

"How will I ever keep it dusted?" said Gramma.

The interior of the mansion was even less inviting.

"This place is creakier than my lower back," said Grampa.

We were greeted by a large, proud woman with a handsome beard. "Greetings, I am Maid Swartwood. Please don't touch anything. Some of these cobwebs are over a hundred years old and are quite valuable."

In the parlor, Maid Swartwood introduced us to a smarmy-looking lawyer.

"Okay, folks," said the lawyer. "So here's the deelio. I shall now read from the will of Lord Clifford "Spanky" Rankonstink, then I will follow up with a song and, perhaps, a few knock-knock jokes."

The Lawyer read from the will.

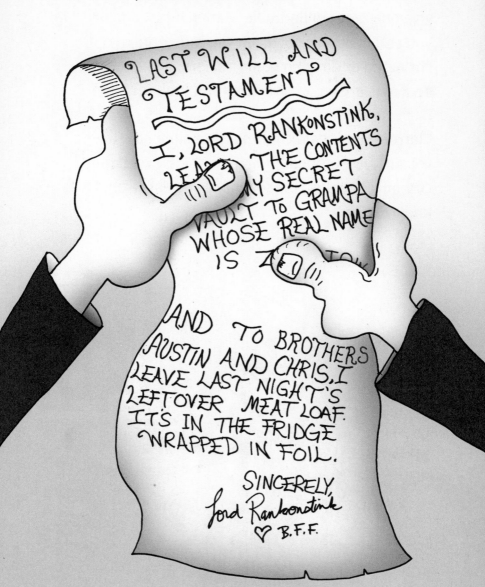

"There is a catch," said the lawyer. "You must survive one night in Badtable Manor. If just one of you can make it until dawn without running out shrieking or dirtying your drawers, the vault's contents are yours. Prepare for a night of terror!"

"Terror! Hah!" said Grampa. "I've climbed a live volcano, I've battled hungry zombies, I've eaten Gramma's cookin' for seventy-five years—oh, I know terror."

CHAPTER 4

Brain Food

Before bed, we had a deluxe, barf-inducing dinner.

"Tonight's special," said Maid Swartwood. "Bulgarian braised brains and boiled turkey necks with goat butter."

"Sounds good," said Grampa. "I'm so hungry I could eat a pickled pig's rump."

"You are in luck, sir. That's on the menu, too."

Maid Swartwood showed me and Jubal our quarters for the evening.

"Nighty night, young ones," she said. "This was young Billy's room before he was taken to the asylum. I think you'll find it most comfortable. His beloved collection of clown dolls will watch over you as you slumber."

She shut out the light and left us with the grinning clowns. I just couldn't get to sleep in that bizarro bedroom.

"Jubal," I said. "I don't know about you, but I'd rather go exploring than sleep next to these bug-eyed bozos."

"I was afraid you might say that," said Jubal.

We ventured out into the dark hallway, which gave Merle a chance to try out his new infrared night-vision goggles.

"Do you get the feeling we're being watched?" Jubal asked.

Suddenly we heard a piercing shriek of terror!

"It's all right! It was just me!" screamed Grampa from the bathroom. "This water's colder than a polar bear at a popsicle convention!"

CHAPTER 5

Can You Dig It?

"Whew!" I said. "It was just Grampa. I thought it might be some leathery old monst—"

Suddenly, a leathery old monster jumped out of nowhere! We screamed bloody murder.

"Pardon me. Would you happen to have any skin conditioner?" asked the monster, who actually was just an extra pale, wrinkly human.

"Who are you?!" I said, startled.

"I'm the local grave digger, Barry Dunderdirt. You kids shouldn't be out of your room. This night is cursed. I've already dug graves for four humans and one cat."

"Cool," I said. "You must know a lot about this place. We'll give you some Pork Cracklins for a tour of the joint."

"Sure! Why not?" said the coot.

Barry took us on a tour of Badtable Manor. Every room was either dripping with slime, bursting with bizarre critters, or filled with noxious gas—it reminded me a lot of the school cafeteria.

"Not only is this wretched house cursed by the
spirits of those who died within these putrid
walls," said Barry, "but it doesn't even have digital
cable or a garbage disposal."

Then, all of a sudden, Barry was gone. But on the wall near us hung his portrait.

"According to that painting," I said, "Barry Dunderdirt's been dead for over twenty-five years! We were just talking to . . . his ghost!"

"Let's go back to our room," said Jubal. "Creepy clown dolls don't seem so bad after all."

CHAPTER 6

Send in the Clowns

When we returned to our bedroom, the clown dolls were waiting for us. Unfortunately they were also hovering three feet above the bed and laughing maniacally!

"Oh man!" said Jubal. "Like I needed another reason to hate clowns."

The clowns launched into an impressive trampo-
line attack.

But they had to deal with Merle first. After years
of clawing up Gramma's furniture, Merle proved
to be a master of removing clown stuffing. He
gutted most of the smiling beasties in no time.

One feisty clown nailed Jubal with a pinwheel-throwing star.

"Noooo!" I yelled as Merle and I performed our famous Kitty Twister strike and split the devilish doll in two.

"Jubal!" I screamed. "Speak to me, Jubal!"

"That's it! I'm outta here," said Jubal, sitting up and pulling something out from under his shirt. "If I didn't keep an emergency box of instant mac 'n' cheese tucked under my shirt at all times, I'd be a goner. I'm spending the rest of the night out in the car."

And so it began—Jubal was the first to leave that awful house.

Soon, Gramma was attacked by a mob of line-dancing cockroaches singing selected tunes from *Bugs Over Broadway*.

"As much as I like musical theatre," said Gramma on her way out the door, "I'll be joining Jubal in the car. See you in the morning."

Merle was lured outside with the old piece of string trick. He and Jubal and Gramma were all disqualified! It was up to me to stick it out 'til dawn. Nothing was going to frighten me away.

That was when I met Marty the Mayonnaise Monster. . . .

"Well," I said, "spending the night in the car isn't such a bad thing. I guess we'll never know what was in that mystery safe."

"Wait a minute!" said Jubal. "Where's your Grampa?"

Grampa had slept through everything! The inheritance was his!

"Eeeeyaaaa!" Grampa yawned as he woke up. "Boy, I don't think I've ever had such a restful sleep. I had lovely dreams filled with chipper songs, smiling clowns, and my very own river of mayonnaise."

CHAPTER 7

Heir to the Throne

Maid Swartwood opened the safe and revealed Grampa's inheritance—a 24k gold-plated litter box.

"This was the master's beloved cat, Mr. Spittles's litter box. It's lined with diamonds and pearls, and is equipped with two ice makers and a bun warmer."

Merle passed out with excitement.

"The late Mr. Spittles took many a poopsy in this box," said Swartwood with a tear in her eye.

"I'm sure he did," said Grampa. "I only hope we can use it with the same care and dignity that Mr. Spittles graced it with years ago."

CHAPTER 8

The Dook of Merle

The next day we were back at Grampa's. It sure was good to be in a house that was free of killer clowns and crooning cockroaches.

Merle got back into his rigorous training schedule to prepare for the cat show.

Gramma helped Merle sculpt his body into a ripped, well-oiled show-cat machine.

Merle was on a strict diet of peanut butter and tuna sandwiches, which were loaded with protein and heck on the breath.

"Hey!" I said. "Maybe it's time to try out that new fancy litter box."

"I just did!" said Grampa. "I have to say it's very luxurious in here but a little cramped and stinky."

CHAPTER 9

That's Phenomenomenal!

That night a huge storm raged outside while
Grampa napped. I was busy assembling my new

Destructor water balloon launcher when I got a strange feeling that we were not alone.

A chill crawled up my spine. Suddenly, we heard Gramma scream in the kitchen!

Things just got weirder and weirder at Grampa's house. First, Paco's fishbowl was haunted by the ghost of a dead floater.

Objects hovered mysteriously.

"Heavens to Betsy!" shouted Grampa. "That balloon is floating all by itself!"

Then the vacuum cleaner sprang to life and
came after us.

"Could you at least vacuum under the drapes?"
asked Gramma. "It's filthy under there."

Then, strange claw marks ripped through the
sofa, almost as if an invisible phantom kitty was
on the loose.

CHAPTER 10

The Real Nitty Gritty

And that wasn't the only bit of feline weirdness. Merle's antique litter box was starting to smell even more ripe than usual.

"Pewww!" said Grampa. "What is that odor? Smells like a diaper full of feta cheese!"

Gramma and I bravely attempted to clean out the litter box, but just as we approached it, the box jumped up into the air and out popped a huge, snarling kitty ghost!

"Holy cat chow!" I screamed. "It's the ghost of Mr. Spittles!"

"Maybe we should come back later," said Gramma.

The ghost cat mashed together all of Merle's
stinky kitty clumps to form a massive insect.

"Holy cow!" said Grampa. "It's a giant litterbug!"

The smelly beast grew to a towering ten feet and clutched Grampa in its moist, gritty bug beak!

"All I wanna know is, what on Earth has Merle been eating?" asked Grampa.

Luckily for us, Gramma jumped in with her air freshener and a jumbo pooper scooper.

"Back, you carpet soiler from the nether regions!" yelled Gramma as she hosed it down with melon-scented Whiff.

Mr. Spittles and his buggy friend retreated back into the litter box.

"I think I've got a clump in my throat," said Grampa.

CHAPTER 11

It Was Just the Wind

The next day we called in some experts from the Gingham County Institute of the Paranormal and Downright Weird.

"Hi, there, folks. I'm Dr. Vapor, this is my colleague, Vick, and this is one of the world's greatest psychics, Madame Inuzat. She can get rid of all evil spirits and she's also great at removing tough cranberry juice stains."

"Tell me, child," said Madame Inuzat. "What kind of disturbances plague this house?"

"Well," I said, "ever since we inherited an antique litter box, this joint's been smelling pretty rank."

"Ah, yes," she said. "My Super Snifr 5000 is picking up a horrid stench from beyond the grave. An otherworldly odor like nothing I've ever whiffed."

"Actually, that was just me," said Grampa, leaving the bathroom. "I shouldn't have had that cabbage and kidney bean omelet for breakfast."

Next, they pulled out fancy sound equipment and pressed it up against the wall.

"What are you doing now?" I asked.

"With this equipment I can hear the unhappy spirits trying to communicate with our world," said Madame Inuzat. "Can you hear that? It sounds like the wailing and crying of a lost soul."

"Sorry," said Grampa, sniffling. "That was me again.
I was just reading the ending of *Charlotte's Web*.
That darn pig just breaks my heart every time."

Finally, I showed Madame Inuzat to the litter box, but as we approached, the ground started to rumble and shake.

"The spirits are angry!" screamed Madame Inuzat. "They are creating an earthquake to frighten us away!"

"Oh, that time it was me," said Gramma, dancing
in front of the TV. "I was playing *Dance Dance
Retribution* and I got a little carried away."

"That litter box is a doorway to another dimension," said Madame Inuzat. "We call it a Portal Potty. It has allowed Mr. Spittles and his ghostly friends to cross over into our world."

"How do we send the ghosts back?" asked Jubal.

"This ghost is an odor-based apparition. We must find something that stinks even worse than Mr. Spittles to fire into the portal."

"Why is everyone looking at me?" asked Grampa.

CHAPTER 12

Sock It to Me

I put on my biocontainment suit and removed Grampa's right sock.

"I'm gonna miss that sock," said Grampa. "I've been wearing it since March."

Then we filled the sock with three-year-old sour cream.

Madame Inuzat and Merle loaded the stink bomb into a special rocket launcher.

Then we fired the malodorous missile into the heart of the litter box.

But to our surprise the box sprouted arms, grabbed Grampa's prized tuba off the wall, and used it to deflect the missile back at us!

The soggy sock exploded in Grampa's face.

"I suppose you'll be needing my other sock," said Grampa.

"No time for that!" I yelled. "We'll just get it straight from the source!"

We picked up Grampa and drove him feet first into the door of the litter box like a human battering ram.

"I've never felt so used!" said Grampa as his feet hit the moist litter.

There was an enormous explosion of electricity, odors, and kitty litter particles! We ran for our lives.

Merle was hit with a huge bolt of energy from the box as kitty litter rained down upon us.

"Ooh, what a mess! Maybe I should have put down some plastic first!" shouted Gramma.

It was all over. Mr. Spittles was gone. The litter box appeared and smelled normal. But Merle looked kinda weird. He didn't seem like himself.

"Boy!" Said Grampa. "My feet feel like a couple of hickory smoked hams."

"This litter box is clean," proclaimed Madame Inuzat. "You'll be getting my bill in the mail."

CHAPTER 13

Whatever Possessed You?

The next day, Gramma was off to the cat show with Merle while we cleaned up the house.

"Don't worry, Granny," said Grampa. "We'll get this place spic and span. Now where's my remote?"

As Gramma walked past us with Merle, I caught a whiff of a familiar smell—the scent of Mr. Spittles!

Jubal and I tried to run after Gramma but she was already on her Harley headed for the Gingham County Auditorium.

"Look!" I said. "The ghost of Mr. Spittles is going with them. Our stink missile didn't send that foul ghost back home— it sent him straight into Merle!"

CHAPTER 14

Poltergeezer

"Why would Mr. Spittles want to possess Merle and go to the cat show?" asked Jubal.

"Look at that scroll the ghost grave digger gave us," I said. "We know that 'a gift so foul' is talking about the litter box. It says here 'beware of vengeance's yowl.' Maybe it's talking about Simon Yowl, the celebrity cat show judge."

"Bingo!" screamed the ghost of Barry Dunderdirt as it jumped right out of the scroll. "I thought you kids would never figure it out."

"I know I'm only eight but I think I just had a heart attack," said Jubal.

"What does Mr. Spittles want with Simon Yowl?" I asked.

"Revenge, my boy!" said Dunderdirt.

CHAPTER 15

The Ghost of Gas Passed

"Long ago, back when I was a young man of eighty-three, Mr. Spittles was a finalist in the local cat show and Simon Yowl was the head judge.

"Mr. Spittles was knockin' 'em dead with his talent, his good looks, and his yodeling skills. He was destined to win."

"But later, Mr. Spittles accidentally cut the kitty cheese right in the face of Mr. Yowl. It was the blast heard 'round the world and Simon made fun of him mercilessly."

"Mr. Spittles never got over it. He spent his last days in that cursed litter box waiting for his chance to seek revenge."

"But you kids can stop him using the clues I left you in that beautiful poem."

"But what does **reverse the pin tack** mean?" I asked. "I don't get it."

"I think I know!" said Jubal. "Look, when I write it in reverse, **pin tack** becomes **kcat nip**! It might be spelled funny, but it's telling us we need to use catnip to drive out the evil spirit."

"Kcorrect!" said the grave digger.

"Wait until you can smell the evil before using the catnip. Go now! Before it's too late," said Dunderdirt, leaping off into space. "If you need me again, just use the scroll, or you can always reach me at www.olddeadguy.com."

We had to get to that cat show and save Simon Yowl from Merle, but first we prepared an arsenal of water balloons laced with high-grade catnip. I was ready to put my Destructor water balloon launcher to use.

"Let's do this," said Grampa.

CHAPTER 16

The Whole Kitten Kaboodle

The cat show was bustling with excitement.

Channel Five's Blue Norther announced the event. "Good evening, folks! Tonight's feline festivities are brought to you by Hola Kitty. Don't tell anyone, but I'm wearing Hola Kitty undies now!"

There was a who's who of cat lovers at the show.
We saw the Big Hair Sugar Sisters and their cat,
Babs.

Even criminal masterminds Hans Lotion and his
grandson, Jurgen, were allowed out of the asylum
to show their cat, Poe—under strict supervision,
of course.

I spotted Gramma brushing Merle's luxurious coat across the auditorium.

"Look!" I said. "Merle is staring out at us from his litter box with that evil look on his contorted face!"

"Maybe he's just constipated," said Grampa.

We spotted the snippy Simon Yowl at his judging station.

"What does a guy have to do around here to get a Jasmine tea and a low-fat muffin?" complained Mr. Yowl.

"Sir!" I screamed. "You are in great danger! We've come here to warn y—"

But we were intercepted by Simon's security squad of old cat ladies.

"Step away from the table," said one of them sternly. "No one gets within ten feet, three inches of Mr. Yowl."

"But he's in great danger!"

"Don't give me no lip, sonny! I'm a triple black belt in the art of fanny smackin'!"

"We're too late!"
screamed Grampa.
"The show is starting
and Merle's struttin'
his stuff!"

CHAPTER 17

Soggy Bottoms

We had to act fast. We ran to the back of the auditorium and pulled out the catnip weaponry.

"I've got the launcher," I said. "Who's got the water balloons?"

"I've hidden them where no one can find them," said Grampa, his butt looking oddly lumpy.

Merle got off to a good start. He aced the physical inspection.

He flew through the obstacle course in record time.

His break-dancing skills wowed the judges and caused a few spectators to faint.

And his one-man show of Abe Lincoln: A Man and His Beard won rave reviews and a standing ovation.

We waited for the ghost to show itself.

"This reminds me of fighting in the trenches during the Big One," said Grampa. "We'd lie in wait for hours until we caught a whiff of the enemy and then BLAMMO!"

"You were in World War II?" said Jubal.

"No," said Grampa. "The Big Squirrel Hunt of 1937. I still have flashbacks."

The final event of the night, the evening gown competition, was coming up and tempers were flaring. The Sugar Sisters were taunting Hans and his kitty.

"You call that a gown?" said The Sugar Sisters. "We've seen better gowns on hospital patients!"

"Oh really?" said Hans. "Is zat bag your cat's vearing paper or plastic?"

"Oh, no you didn't!" said the Sisters.

"Bring it, girlfriend!" said Hans.

CHAPTER 18

Reeking Havoc

While the other contestants were bickering, Merle walked out on the catwalk in a stunning Vera Fang gown and put everyone else to shame. He owned the runway.

"Ladies and gentlemen," said Blue Norther. "I think we can just stop the show right now. We have a winner!"

Merle did it! He was swept up and placed on a pedestal. It was a whirlwind of emotion as Blue Norther sang the national cat show theme song, "Two Scoops of Glory."

That's when it happened. Merle let one rip just as Simon was placing the crown on Merle's head.

"Great gossamer's ghost!" said Mr. Yowl. "I haven't smelled anything that foul since . . . No! It couldn't be! Mr. Spittles!"

The ghost of Mr. Spittles laughed at Simon as Merle used his supernatural powers to raise Mr. Yowl and Blue Norther's wig ten feet off the floor.

All heck broke out at the cat show as Merle re-leased hordes of evil cat spirits and blocked all of the exits with a flick of the wrist.

Merle even broke the restraints on Hans and Jurgen and freed the master criminals!

"At last! Freedom!" shouted Hans. "Now ve can take over Gingham County. But first, ve go to Denny's. I vant me a Grand Slam Breakfast!"

It was complete chaos in the auditorium. Chairs and kitties were flying. Water hoses writhed around like giant anacondas.

Cat ghosts screamed through the air as people levitated above the ground. It was a good time.

"Hey, stinko! Your hauntin' days are over!" yelled Grampa as he flung the first catnip water balloon.

But the balloon just passed right through the ghost and nailed Fran Calhoon's big hair instead.

Then Merle used his ghostly powers to bring the forty-foot-tall Hola Kitty statue to life! It ripped free from its pedestal and stomped toward us.

"Run, people!" I screamed. "Don't be fooled by its cute whiskers and pink dress. It's lethal!"

And then, the icing on the cake—Hola Kitty started to breathe fire.

Simon's granny security team tried to challenge the behemoth, but one breath from the kitty filled the air with the smell of singed wigs.

CHAPTER 19

Try Some Nasal Spray

"I've got an idea!" said Jubal as he grabbed the balloons and started sucking out the contents.

"Jubal!" I screamed. "You shouldn't be drinking that nasty catnip water!"

"Yeah!" said Grampa. "This is no time to be snacking."

But Jubal didn't swallow it. He had something else in mind.

We climbed up a ladder to the jumbo-tron monitor.

"Hey, change the channel while you're up there!" said Grampa. "There's a good ball game on Channel Twelve."

Hola Kitty was just about to step on Mr. Yowl
while Grampa tried to drag him to safety.

"I'm sorry, Mr. Spittles!" screamed Simon. "I never
meant to offend you. I've always said of all the
terrible odors I've smelled, yours was the most
impressive!"

"Mmmmphhh! Mmmmmphhh!" yelled Jubal
which translated to "Hey! Whisker brain! Up
here!"

We grabbed a cat show banner, flung it over the
rafters, and jumped off the jumbo-tron.

We swung over the angry kitty and Jubal used his world famous nostril milk shooting ability to hose Mr. Spittles down with the catnip solution.

The catnip drove Mr. Spittles back into his box. In fact, Jubal was able to use his double blaster nostril skills to round up most of the ghosts and send them back into the litter box.

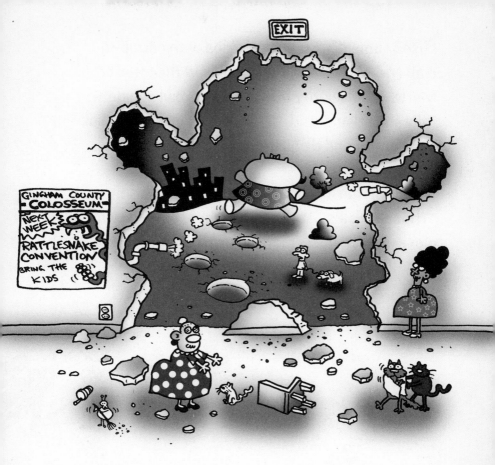

Unfortunately, the giant Hola Kitty managed to escape by crashing through the wall and taking off through Gingham County Park.

"Oh, boy," said Grampa. "That's gonna freak out some joggers."

I used some duct tape sprinkled with catnip to trap Mr. Spittles and his buddies in the litter box. Merle was back to normal, Simon Yowl accidentally smiled and said, "Thanks," and Gramma was both proud and disgusted by Jubal's nasal skills.

Blue Norther brought the night to a close. "That's it folks. Another cat show comes to a close. Join us next month for the mummified pitbull convention."

CHAPTER 20

That's a Wrap!

We returned the golden litter box to Badtable Manor. It turns out Grampa really wasn't related to Lord Rankonstink after all.

"We just wanted to get rid of Mr. Spittles' ghost," said Maid Swartwood. "He's a real drag."

"Well," said Grampa, " I should be mad but I can't blame you for trying, sister."

So that's the scoop. We ended up getting Merle a fancy new litter box with a self-cleaning droid, central air, and no sign of evil spirits whatsoever.

We managed to round up most of the escaped ghosts, but Gramma decided to keep her haunted, hands-free vacuum.

Jubal and I used grave digger Barry to scare our friends and teachers. He was a big hit at parties.

As for the giant Hola Kitty, no one's seen it for sure since it escaped . . .

But rumor has it, it's huge in Japan.

CRACKPOT SNAPSHOT

Two portraits painted by Vincent Van Rembrain were discovered in the basement of Badtable Manor. Experts say they're authentic, but that second one looks like a fake to me. Help us pick out the differences and determine which painting is precious and which is just plain putrid.

The answers are on the next page. Anyone caught cheating will have to eat a kitty clump corn muffin with a side of creamed spinach!

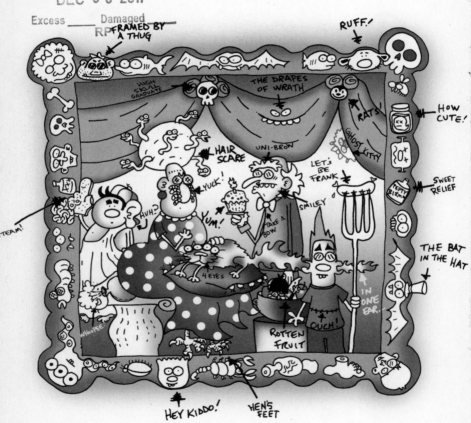